Adapted by Kristen Depken

A Random House PICTUREBACK® Book
Random House 🏠 New York

Copyright © 2008 Disney Enterprises, Inc. All rights reserved. Published in the United States by Random House Children's Books, a division of Random House, Inc., 1745 Broadway, New York, NY 10019, and in Canada by Random House of Canada Limited, Toronto, in conjunction with Disney Enterprises, Inc. Pictureback, Random House, and the Random House colophon are registered trademarks of Random House, Inc.

Library of Congress Control Number: 2007938819   ISBN: 978-0-375-85203-9

www.randomhouse.com/kids/disney

Printed in the United States of America

10 9 8 7 6 5 4

First Edition

Atlantica was a magical kingdom under the sea. Ruled by kindhearted King Triton and Queen Athena, it was full of music, laughter, and happy merpeople.

The king and queen had seven little daughters. Queen Athena loved music, and every night, she sang the princesses a lullaby just for them. The youngest, Ariel, especially adored her mother's singing.

One day, while the royal family enjoyed an outing in a cove above the waves, King Triton surprised his wife with a music box that played her special lullaby.

Queen Athena loved the gift.

Suddenly, a dark shadow fell over the royal family—a pirate ship!
King Triton rushed the princesses to safety. But Queen Athena had left her
music box behind, on the rocks!

She raced back to get it.

The king looked on helplessly as the queen was lost forever.

Heartbroken, King Triton threw the music box out to sea. He blamed
music for what had happened to Queen Athena—and banned music from
Atlantica forever!

Ten years later, the kingdom looked almost the same . . . but it did not feel the same. Music was still forbidden, and King Triton had become very strict. He didn't like any kind of surprises, especially from his daughters.

Meanwhile, Princess Ariel had grown into a beautiful and spirited mermaid. She disliked her father's daily routines and preferred to go on adventures.

All the princesses were taken care of by their ambitious governess, Marina Del Rey. But Marina didn't like looking after the princesses. She had other plans—she wanted to be King Triton's chief of staff. Unfortunately, that position was held by the wise crab Sebastian.

"I deserve that job," Marina complained to her assistant, Benjamin. She began to think of ways she could take over Sebastian's duties.

One day, Ariel disrupted the family's daily swim by tickling her sisters with seaweed. King Triton was not pleased.

"You have to learn to respect the way I run this kingdom," he scolded Ariel.

As punishment, King Triton made Ariel scrape barnacles all day. While she was working, she heard a tuneful *bop-bop-bop-de-bop!* A blue and yellow fish named Flounder was playing the coral tubes.

"Can you do that again?" the Little Mermaid asked.

Suddenly, two palace swordfish appeared. "Halt!" one guard said. "All music is forbidden in the kingdom."

Luckily, Ariel helped Flounder escape, and the two became fast friends.

That night, Ariel spotted Flounder swimming past her bedroom window. Curious, she secretly followed him through the kelp forest . . . to a hidden nightclub called the Catfish Club!

Ariel couldn't believe her eyes and ears. Onstage, a band was playing a lively calypso song. Then the star of the show appeared. It was Sebastian!

"You never saw this!" the crab told Ariel as he hurried away. He knew music was forbidden, and he was worried that Ariel would tell her father about the club.

"No, wait, I won't tell!" cried Ariel. But everyone swam off and hid.

Alone, Ariel felt disappointed and frustrated. Her tail accidentally brushed against a bass string. She loved the sound! Soon she was playing the instruments and singing.

Flounder, Sebastian, and the band came out from hiding when they heard the Little Mermaid's beautiful voice. Realizing how much Ariel loved music, Sebastian made her take the musician's oath: "Do you promise to jump, jive, wail, groove, rock steady, and at all times lend a helping hand to your fellow music lovers?"

"I do!" Ariel promised.

The next day, Ariel's sisters found out about her secret adventure. They wanted to go to the club, too. So that night, Ariel took them to the Catfish Club.

The princesses were having so much fun that they didn't notice someone spying on them. It was Marina Del Rey—and she couldn't wait to report everything to King Triton. He was furious! "I will not have music in my kingdom!" he shouted.

King Triton destroyed the Catfish Club. Then he had Sebastian, Flounder, and the band thrown in jail. Just as she had planned, Marina became the new chief of staff.

Ariel felt very sad when she saw her friends behind bars. So she secretly freed Sebastian, Flounder, and the band.

"Without music, this place just isn't home," Ariel told them.

Together, they all decided to run away and never return to Atlantica.

Back at the palace, King Triton discovered that Ariel and Sebastian were missing. He was worried and ordered his guards to find them and bring them back. But if Sebastian returned, Marina thought she might lose her new job.

"What are you going to do?" asked Benjamin.

"Whatever it takes to get rid of Sebastian!" said Marina.

"But what about Ariel?" Benjamin replied.

"You're right: she'll tattle. I'll have to get rid of her, too." With her evil pet eels, Marina set out after Ariel and Sebastian.

Far from Atlantica, Ariel spotted something shining in the rocks at the bottom of the sea. It was her mother's music box, from so many years ago!

"When your mother died, the whole kingdom was heartbroken," Sebastian told Ariel. "The heart that never healed was your father's."

"He's forgotten what it feels like to be happy," said Ariel. "I have to bring this back to him."

Ariel, Flounder, and Sebastian decided to return to Atlantica.
Along the way, they swam right into Marina and her eels!

"Sic 'em, boys," said Marina, who was dressed in full battle gear.

The friends tried to escape, but they were surrounded.

Luckily, the rest of the band arrived just in time! They had remembered their oath to always help out a fellow musician.

"I've won!" Sebastian yelled as he trapped Marina inside a coral tube.

"This is not over!" shouted Marina. She toppled her tube and rocketed down the hill—straight toward the little crab!

Ariel quickly jumped in front of her friend to protect him, but she was knocked into a deep ravine.

Just then, King Triton arrived. Seeing his daughter in danger, he rushed down to save her.

As King Triton lifted the unconscious Ariel into his arms, the music box fell from her hand and began to play. King Triton remembered how happy his family used to be. He softly sang the queen's lullaby to his daughter.

"I'm so sorry I didn't listen," King Triton told the Little Mermaid.

Ariel slowly opened her eyes and hugged her father. "Daddy, let's go home."

After everyone returned to Atlantica, King Triton took the musician's oath.

"I hereby decree that music will once again ring clear from one end of my kingdom to the other!" King Triton announced. Everyone cheered!

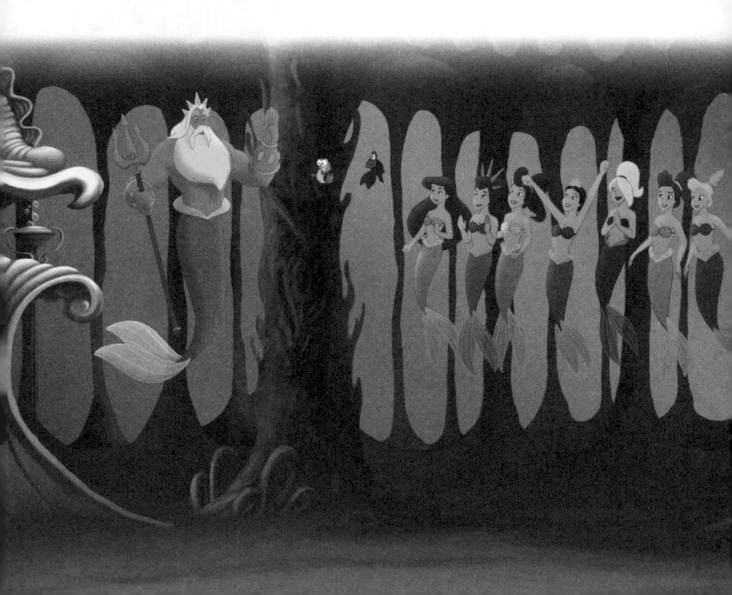

Ariel couldn't have been happier! The whole kingdom celebrated with music, dancing, and laughter.

Locked away in the dungeon, even Benjamin couldn't keep from dancing!